Geronimo Stilton
ENGLISH!

14 TOGETHER AT THE PARK 一起去公園

U0099997

新雅文化事業有限公司
www.sunya.com.hk

Geronimo Stilton English
TOGETHER AT THE PARK　一起去公園

作　　者：Geronimo Stilton 謝利連摩·史提頓
譯　　者：申倩
責任編輯：王燕參
封面繪圖：Giuseppe Facciotto
插圖繪畫：Claudio Cernuschi, Andrea Denegri, Daria Cerchi
內文設計：Angela Ficarelli, Raffaella Picozzi
出　　版：新雅文化事業有限公司
　　　　　香港筲箕灣耀興道3號東匯廣場9樓
　　　　　營銷部電話：（852）2562 0161
　　　　　客戶服務部電話：（852）2976 6559
　　　　　傳真：（852）2597 4003
　　　　　網址：http://www.sunya.com.hk
　　　　　電郵：marketing@sunya.com.hk
發　　行：香港聯合書刊物流有限公司
　　　　　香港新界大埔汀麗路36號中華商務印刷大廈3字樓
　　　　　電話：（852）2150 2100　　傳真：（852）2407 3062
　　　　　電郵：info@suplogistics.com.hk
印　　刷：C & C Offset Printing Co.,Ltd
　　　　　香港新界大埔汀麗路36號
版　　次：二〇一一年六月初版
　　　　　10 9 8 7 6 5 4 3 2 1

ISBN: 978-962-08-5370-8
© 2007 Edizioni Piemme S.p.A., Via Tiziano 32 - 20145 Milano - Italia
International Rights © 2007 Atlantyca S.p.A. - via Leopardi, 8, Milano - Italy
© 2011 for this Work in Traditional Chinese language, Sun Ya Publications (HK) Ltd.
9/F, Eastern Central Plaza, 3 Yiu Hing Rd, Shau Kei Wan, Hong Kong
Published and printed in Hong Kong

CONTENTS
目錄

BENJAMIN'S CLASSMATES
班哲文的老師和同學們

Maestra Topitilla
托比蒂拉・德・托比莉斯

Rarin
拉琳

Diego
迪哥

Rupa
露芭

Tui
杜爾

David
大衛

Sakura
櫻花

Mohamed
穆哈麥德

Tian Kai
田凱

Oliver
奧利佛

Milenko
米蘭哥

Trippo
特里普

Carmen
卡敏

Atina
阿提娜

Esmeralda
愛絲梅拉達

Pandora
潘朵拉

Takeshi
北野

Kuti
菊花

Benjamin
班哲文

Hsing
阿星

Laura
羅拉

Kiku
奇哥

Antonia
安東妮婭

Liza
麗莎

GERONIMO AND HIS FRIENDS
謝利連摩和他的家鼠朋友們

謝利連摩・史提頓 Geronimo Stilton

一個古怪的傢伙,簡直可以說是一隻笨拙的文化鼠。他是《鼠民公報》的總裁,正花盡心思改變報紙業的歷史。

菲・史提頓 Tea Stilton

謝利連摩的妹妹,她是《鼠民公報》的特派記者,同時也是一個運動愛好者。

班哲文・史提頓 Benjamin Stilton

謝利連摩的小侄兒,常被叔叔稱作「我的小乳酪」,是一隻感情豐富的小老鼠。

潘朵拉・華之鼠 Pandora Woz

柏蒂・活力鼠的姨甥女、班哲文最好的朋友,是一隻活潑開朗的小老鼠。

柏蒂・活力鼠 Patty Spring

美麗迷人的電視新聞工作者,致力於她熱愛的電視事業。

賴皮 Trappola

謝利連摩的表弟,非常喜歡食物,風趣幽默,是一隻饞嘴、愛開玩笑的老鼠,善於將歡樂傳遞給每一隻鼠。

麗萍姑媽 Zia Lippa

謝利連摩的姑媽,對鼠十分友善,又和藹可親,只想將最好的給身邊的鼠。

艾拿 Iena

謝利連摩的好朋友,充滿活力,熱愛各項運動,他希望能把對運動的熱誠傳給謝利連摩。

史奎克・愛管閒事鼠 Ficcanaso Squitt

謝利連摩的好朋友,是一個非常有頭腦的私家偵探,總是穿着一件黃色的乾濕褸。

LET'S GO TO THE PARK!
一起到公園去！

親愛的小朋友，你知道我的工作很忙。幸好我的小侄兒班哲文和潘朵拉偶爾要我陪他們到公園去玩，這樣散散步不但對身體好（當然我本身並不是一隻運動型的老鼠），而且對頭腦也很好（而我的頭腦平時總是想着太多的事情）。我以一千塊莫澤雷勒乳酪發誓，在公園裏散步真的很開心，我決定以後每天都要來公園走走看看……你也跟我一起來吧！

I'm Going to the Park

Today I'm going to the park to have a picnic,
I'll eat my good cheesecake and I'll dance with my friends.
1 2 3 4, stand, jump, left and right, up and down,
clap your hands. Do you want to dance with me?

6

跟我謝利連摩·史提頓一起學英文，
就像玩遊戲一樣簡單好玩！

你可以一邊看着圖畫一邊讀。
以下有幾個標誌，你要特別留意：

當看到 標誌時，你可以聽CD，
一邊聽，一邊跟着朗讀，還可以跟
着一起唱歌。

當看到 ★ 標誌時，你可以和朋友
們一起玩遊戲，或者嘗試回答問
題。題目很簡單，它們對鞏固你所
學過的內容很有幫助。

當看到 ❶ 標誌時，你要注意看一
下格子裏的生字，反覆唸幾遍，掌
握發音。

最後，不要忘記完成小測驗和練習
冊裏的問題！看看你有多聰明吧。

祝大家學得開開心心！

謝利連摩·史提頓

7

晴天的時候，最適合去公園散步了。很多老鼠朋友們跟我、班哲文和潘朵拉都有着同樣的想法……因此，班哲文和潘朵拉在公園裏碰到很多好朋友！他們還在公園裏看到很多不同的事物，這些事物用英語該怎麼說呢？你可以跟他們一起說說看。

on	在……上面
up there	在那兒上面
over there	在那邊

Look at all those red berries!

Where?

On that bush!

red berry

sparrow

bush

Look at all those daisies!

Where?

Over there!

gravel

path

grass

daisy

答案：
1.That is a sparrow.
2.Look at all those daisies.

9

LET'S PLAY! 一起玩吧！

天氣好熱啊！我決定到樹蔭下的長椅上坐下來休息一下，而班哲文和朋友們則在草地上玩球……

看看他們在說什麼？你也跟着一起說說看。

Yes, throw the ball in the air.

May I play with you?

Trippo can throw the ball in the air.

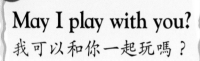

May I play with you?

我可以和你一起玩嗎？

I'm not very good at ball games.

Don't worry. Try to do your best!

Atina is not very good at ball games.

Where is the ball?

Over there, in the bush!

⭐ 請用英語說出：「我可以和你一起玩嗎？」

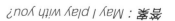
答案：May I play with you?

10

WHERE IS THE BALL?
球在哪裏？

班哲文和朋友們在一起玩球，但是玩着玩着，球不知道滾到哪裏去了？請你幫忙一起找找看。

next to

The ball is next to the bush.

behind

The ball is behind the bush.

between

The ball is between the bush and the tree.

next to 在……旁邊
behind 在……後面
between 在……之間

Play Football with Me!

I like going on the swing
it feels like flying.
I love going on the slide
when I am in this park.
I climb on the rope-bridge
and I feel so brave.
I play in the wendy house
just like the Indians,
but the thing I like most
is playing... football!
I OH I OH I OH
I like playing football!
I OH I OH I OH
Let's play football together!
I OH I OH I OH
When you play football.
you make many friends.
I OH I OH I OH
And then all together
we eat an ice cream!
We have a good time!
We have a good time!

I OH I OH I OH
We have a good time!

THAT'S FUN!　真有趣！

　　公園裏有很多不同的遊樂設施，班哲文和拉琳一看見鞦韆，馬上跑過去玩。而阿提娜和大衞則去溜冰場玩滾軸溜冰，他們要比賽誰先滑到我身邊呢。各就各位，預備⋯⋯開始！

1 Rarin is on the swing.
Benjamin is behind her and he
is pushing her.
The swing goes to and fro.
Now Rarin is near Benjamin...
Now she is far from him...

2 Pandora goes near the swing
to say hello to Benjamin and
Rarin.

3 Atina and David
are skating towards
Geronimo.

!
to and fro	來回
near	近
far	遠
towards	向着
along	沿着

4 Hsing is skating
towards the centre
of the skating rink.

5 Tian Kai
is skating
along the
edge of
the skating
rink.

PARK RULES AND REGULATIONS 公園裏的規則

公園是讓大家休憩的地方，每個人都應該遵守公園裏的規則。現在就讓我們一起來看看下面的圖片，了解一下在公園裏有哪些規則要遵守吧！

1 Throw rubbish into litter bin.

2 Don't pick flowers.

3 Not drinking water.

⭐ 你知道在公園裏要遵守哪些規則嗎？請用英語說出其中一項。

4 No motorcycles.

Do not throw rubbish into the bush!

He gets a fine!

THE SWAN POND 天鵝池

公園裏還有一個池塘，這裏住着許多不同種類的動物。班哲文和潘朵拉正在池塘的另一邊玩遙控船，希望他們玩的時候，不會打擾到動物們的生活。

willow

bridge

remote-controlled toy boat

duckling

cygnet

duck

swan

water lily

frog

stone

fish

pond

sand

The pond is full of water lilies.

Look! The cygnets are on mother swan's back.

The ducklings are swimming in a line, behind mother duck.

★ 用英語說出以下的詞彙：
池塘、沙、石頭。

14

答案：pond, sand, stone.

LET'S KEEP FIT!
一起來健身！

接着，班哲文和潘朵拉又帶我到公園裏玩健身的地方，我以一千塊莫澤雷勒乳酪發誓，我真的很不想留在這裏。可是孩子們還是說服我至少要試試平衡木，真的難以形容我在平衡木上頭暈目眩有多痛苦！

Benjamin is touching his toes ten times.

Pandora is doing exercises for her tummy muscles on the bench.

Sakura is jumping, opening and closing her arms and legs.

Milenko is running backwards and forwards: he's really fit.

Can you help me, Benjamin? Please!

Help me, Pandora!

Geronimo is walking on the balance beam and... he's afraid of heights.

GAMES FOR TWO 二人遊戲

艾拿也在公園裏鍛煉身體，就像平常一樣。當他看到我的時候，他非常高興，還邀請我跟他一起跑步。可是我太累了，於是艾拿就跟小朋友們玩遊戲：由他當主持人，發號施令，讓孩子們比賽做運動，誰做得好誰就可以得到一分！

Pandora, Trippo: bend forwards ten times. Ready? Go!

One point for Pandora.

Mohamed, Sakura: do ten series of exercises for your tummy muscles. Ready, Go!

One point for Mohamed.

One point for Atina.

Kiku, Atina: jump, opening and closing your arms and legs. Ready? Go!

Rarin, Diego: run backwards and forwards. Ready? Go!

One point for Diego.

AT THE BOOTH 小食亭

做了這麼多運動之後，真是要好好補充一下體力了，於是我提議大家一起到小食亭去吃點東西，我請客喇！

> May I have a sandwich, please?

> I want a yoghurt and some orange juice.

> And a bottle of water... thank you!

> I would like a slice of strawberry pie.

booth	小食亭	yoghurt	酸乳酪
waiter	侍應	strawberry pie	士多啤梨批
drinks	飲品	strawberries	士多啤梨
orange juice	橙汁	strawberries and cream	士多啤梨忌廉
sandwich	三文治	water	水

ALPHABET-BALL 字母球

玩了這麼久，是時候回家了，不過在回去之前孩子們還要跟我玩最後一個遊戲！

遊戲玩法：

1. 主持人首先把球拋向空中，同時說：「Alphabet-ball says…」，他必須說出一個字母，比如說A。
2. 其他參加者便要爭取在球落地之前接到球，接到球的參加者要同時說出一個以字母A作開頭的詞彙，比如說APPLE。
3. 如果他說對了，就可以得到一分；如果他說錯了或說不出來，就要把球拋還給主持人，重新開始一輪遊戲。
4. 最後誰得的分數最多便算贏。

19

〈會「飛」的社論〉

在妙鼠城的城市公園裏。

謝利連摩：為什麼我會決定在公園裏寫這篇社論呢？

謝利連摩：這篇「妙鼠城的乳酪消耗量」，我足足寫了4小時啊！

謝利連摩：但是，就在短短兩秒鐘內它被一陣強風吹走了，它在哪裏呢？真丟臉啊！如果……

謝利連摩：……被馬克思爺爺——《鼠民公報》的前總裁在這裏見到我的話。
馬克思：謝利連摩，我知道我是誰。
潘朵拉：謝利連摩叔叔，你在做什麼？
謝利連摩：我……呀……我正在跨上搖木馬……

謝利連摩：……這樣才能騎呀！
馬克思：你沒事吧？

謝利連摩：哦，我沒事！做回小朋友的感覺真是太好了！

謝利連摩：我的文稿！在那裏！
謝利連摩（心裏想）：我一定要追到那些文稿，但不能被他們發現。

謝利連摩：再做一些健康的緩步跑，保持年輕。

天娜：他沒事吧？

謝利連摩（心裏想）：我快抓到那些文稿了。

謝利連摩：啊哈！

半小時後……

謝利連摩：它們在這裏！

謝利連摩：好極了了了了！

菲：謝利連摩，爺爺很擔心你呀！
班哲文：你怎樣了？
馬克思：你上一次放假是什麼時候？

謝利連摩：噢，我不需要放假。我剛剛才寫完我的社論……

馬克思：哦，你那篇一定不會比我十年前寫的那篇好。

馬克思：它令我得到此生的第一個獎呢！那篇文章的題目叫做「妙鼠城的乳酪消耗量」！呀，這些紙張是用來做什麼的？

The End

謝利連摩：沒什麼……或許我真的需要一個假期……

TEST 小測驗

⭐ 1. 「我們一起去公園吧！」用英語該怎麼説？選出正確的句子，大聲讀出來。

Let's go to the park!

I'm going to the park.

⭐ 2. 用英語説出下面有關植物的詞彙。

> 樹　　　樹枝　　　樹葉　　　灌木叢　　　花

⭐ 3. 看看圖畫，用英語説出下面的動物名稱。

天鵝	青蛙	鴨子	小鴨子

⭐ 4. 用英語説出下面的食物名稱。

> 士多啤梨　　　　士多啤梨忌廉　　　　士多啤梨批

⭐ 5. 用英語説出下面的句子。

(a) 不用擔心，試着盡力做好它！
Don't worry. Try to ... ...

(b) 拉琳坐在鞦韆上。
Rarin is ... ...

(c) 潘朵拉正在長椅上做仰臥起坐。
Pandora is doing ... ... for her ... ... on the ...

(d) 櫻花正在做一邊跳，一邊張開、合攏雙手雙腿的運動。
Sakura is jumping ... ... and ... her ... and ...

Track 4
（英、粵、普發聲）

DICTIONARY 詞典

A

along　沿着

arms　手臂

B

back　背

backwards　向後

balance beam　平衡木

ball games　球類運動

banks　岸

behind　在……後面

bench　長椅

bend　彎腰

between　在……之間

bird　小鳥

booth　小食亭

branch　樹枝

brave　勇敢

bridge　橋

bush　灌木叢

C

centre　中心

cheese　乳酪

city　城市

climb　爬

consumption　消耗量

cygnet　小天鵝

D

daisy　雛菊

decide　決定

director　總裁

down　下

drinks　飲品

duck　鴨子

duckling　小鴨子

E

edge 邊緣

exercises 運動

F

far 遠

fine 罰款

fish 魚

flower 花

flying 飛

football 足球

forwards 向前

friends 朋友

frog 青蛙

G

good at 善於

grandpa 爺爺

grass 草

gravel 碎石

H

hands 手

healthy 健康的

help 幫助

holiday 假期

I

ice cream 雪糕

islet 小島

J

jogging 緩步跑

jump 跳

K

keep fit 健身

L

lawn 草地

leaf 葉子

left 左

legs 腿

M

motorcycles

電單車（普：摩托車）

muscles　肌肉

N

near　近

need　需要

next to　在⋯⋯旁邊

O

on　在⋯⋯上面

orange juice　橙汁

over there　在那邊

P

papers　紙張

park　公園

path　小徑

pick　摘

picnic　野餐

play　玩

pond　池塘

R

race　比賽

red berry　紅莓

reeds　蘆葦

remote-controlled toy boat

遙控玩具船

ride　騎

right　右

rope-bridge　繩橋

rubbish　垃圾

S

sand　沙

sandwich

三文治（普：三明治）

skating rink　溜冰場

slide　滑梯

sparrow　麻雀

stand　站立

strawberry pie　士多啤梨批
　（普：草莓派）

stone　石頭

stuck　被困住

swan　天鵝

swing　鞦韆

T

throw　拋

to and fro　來回

today　今天

toes　腳趾

together　一起

towards　向着

tree　樹

trunk　樹幹

try　嘗試

tummy　肚子

U

underwater　水下的

up　上

up there　在那兒上面

W

waiter　侍應

walk　走路

water lily　荷花

willow　柳樹

wind　風

Y

yoghurt　酸乳酪

young　年輕

28

看在一千塊莫澤雷勒乳酪的份上，你學得開心嗎？很開心，對不對？好極了！跟你一起跳舞唱歌我也很開心！我等着你下次繼續跟班哲文和潘朵拉一起玩一起學英語呀。現在要說再見了，當然是用英語說啦！

GERONIMO'S ISLAND
老鼠島地圖

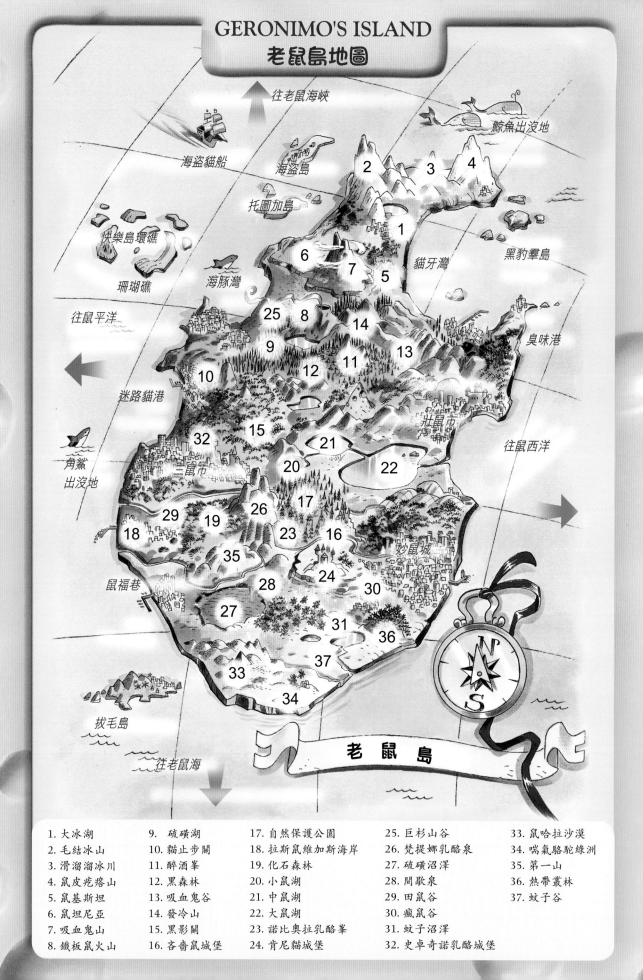

往老鼠海峽

鯨魚出沒地

海盜貓船

海盜島

托圖加島

2　3　4

黑豹羣島

快樂島環礁

6

1

珊瑚礁　　海豚灣

7　　貓牙灣

往鼠平洋

25　8

5

14

臭味港

9

13

10

12

11

莊鼠市

迷路貓港

15

32

21

往鼠西洋

20

22

二鼠市

17

角鯊
出沒地

29　19　26

23　16

妙鼠城

18

35

24

30

鼠福巷

28

27

31

36

33

37

34

拔毛島

往老鼠海

老鼠島

Geronimo Stilton

EXERCISE BOOK

練習冊

想知道自己對 TOGETHER AT THE PARK 掌握了多少，
趕快打開後面的練習完成它吧！

ENGLISH!

14 TOGETHER AT THE PARK　一起去公園

A WALK IN THE PARK
在公園裏散步

⭐ 謝利連摩和小朋友們在公園裏看到很多不同的事物，這些事物用英語該怎麼説呢？把代表答案的英文字母寫在 ☐ 內。

A. daisy　　F. bush
B. trunk　　G. bird
C. branch　　H. bench
D. leaf　　I. path
E. grass　　J. flower

WHERE IS THE BALL?
球在哪裏？

⭐ 從下面選出正確的詞彙填在橫線上，完成句子。

behind	between	next to

1. The ball is _____ the bush.

2. The ball is _____ the bush.

3. The ball is _____ the bush and the tree.

2

PARK RULES AND REGULATIONS
公園裏的規則

⭐ 你知道在公園裏要遵守哪些規則嗎？根據圖畫，從下面選出適當的句子，把代表答案的英文字母填在 ☐ 內。

A. Throw rubbish into litter bin.
B. Don't pick flowers.
C. Not drinking water.
D. No motorcycles.

1.

2.

3.

4.

THE SWAN POND 天鵝池

⭐ 班哲文和他的朋友們在天鵝池看到很多不同的事物，這些事物用英語該怎麼說呢？把代表答案的英文字母寫在 □ 內。

A. willow   B. swan   C. cygnet
D. duck   E. duckling   F. frog
G. fish   H. bridge

THE REMOTE-CONTROLLED TOY BOATS 遙控玩具船

⭐ 謝利連摩、班哲文和潘朵拉正在玩遙控玩具船。根據下面的描述，判斷下圖中的小船是屬於誰的，在橫線上寫出正確的答案。

Benjamin's boat is near the banks of the pond.

Pandora's boat goes far away, near the islet.

Geronimo's boat is stuck in the reeds.

1. _____ boat

2. _____ boat

3. _____ boat

LET'S KEEP FIT!
一起來健身！

⭐ 看看下面的圖畫，他們正在做什麼運動呢？把圖畫和相應的句子用線連起來。

1.

A. Benjamin is touching his toes ten times.

2.

B. Pandora is doing exercises for her tummy muscles on the bench.

3.

C. Sakura is jumping, opening and closing her arms and legs.

4.

D. Milenko is running backwarks and forwards: he's really fit!

AT THE BOOTH 小食亭

⭐ 從下面選出適當的英文詞彙，填在圖畫下面的橫線上。

booth   orange juice   sandwich   yoghurt
strawberry pie   strawberries   water

1.

_____

2.

_____

3.

_____

4.

_____

5.

_____

6.

_____

7.

_____

ANSWERS 答案

TEST 小測驗

1. Let's go to the park!

2. tree / trees ; branch / branches ; leaf / leaves ; bush / bushes ; flower / flowers

3. swan; frog; duck; ducklings

4. strawberry / strawberries ; strawberries and cream ; strawberry pie

5. (a) Don't worry. Try to <u>do your best</u>!   (b) Rarin is <u>on the swing</u>.

   (c) Pandora is doing <u>exercises</u> for her <u>tummy muscles</u> on the <u>bench</u>.

   (d) Sakura is jumping, <u>opening</u> and <u>closing</u> her <u>arms</u> and <u>legs</u>.

EXERCISE BOOK 練習冊

P.1

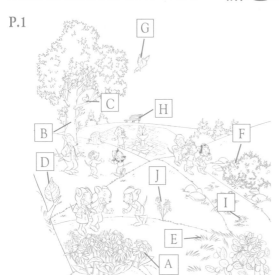

P.4

P.2

1. next to   2. behind   3. between

P.3

1. D   2. A   3. B   4. C

P.5

1. Pandora's   2. Geronimo's   3. Benjamin's

P.6

1. D   2. A   3. C   4. B

P.7

1. booth   2. water   3. orange juice   4. sandwich

5. strawberries   6. yoghurt   7. strawberry pie